Brum™

BRUM AND THE FIRE ENGINE

Written by Lesley Young
Illustrated by Robin Davies

PictureLions

An Imprint of HarperCollins*Publishers*

It was Brum's day for exploring the big town.

He was brum brum brumming his way past the fire station when SPLASH! he was covered in a bucketful of dirty water. The firemen were so busy cleaning the engine, they didn't see their friend Brum.

"Oops – sorry, Brum," shouted a fireman. "Stay where you are and we'll soon have you clean again."

The firemen fetched buckets of soapy water and began to rub Brum all over. Soon he was hidden in a thick cloud of bubbles.

When he was squeaky clean, Brum beep-beeped his thanks and brummed off down the pavement.

Further down the road, a balloon seller was holding a huge bunch of balloons. A little girl had saved up all her pocket money to buy one.

"Let me tie it to your dolly for you," said the balloon seller, "and then you won't lose it."

"What a good idea," thought Brum.

"Wait for me," he beeped, brumming down the pavement after the little girl.

The little girl skipped happily along. But two big bullies were watching her.

"Let's see your balloon," said one.

"Yeah! And let's see your doll," said the other.

One of them snatched the doll away and the other one began to pull at the balloon string.

Brum speeded up and screeched to a halt beside them.

"What do you think you're doing?" he said.

The bullies were so surprised to see Brum they let go of the doll and the balloon.

At once the balloon soared up into the sky, carrying the doll higher and higher.

"Ha! Ha!" screeched the nasty boy and girl, holding their sides with laughter. "You'll never get them back now!"

The little girl was so angry she forgot to be frightened.

"You bully!" she shouted and she slapped the boy as hard as she could.

The boy dropped his bag of toffees and when he bent down to pick them up, Brum brummed up behind him and butted him like a goat.

"Come on," said Brum to the little girl, "let's follow your balloon."

They rushed down the pavement, past a man cleaning his car. "It went that way…"

Brum brum brum went the little car, run run run went the little girl.

"Look!" cried the little girl at last, pointing upwards. The string of the balloon had wound itself around a satellite dish on the top of a high building.

Brum felt dizzy just looking at it.

Brum knew there was only one thing to do.

He brummed into the building and drove right up to the roof. He saw the balloon floating in the sky just ahead of him.

Brum raced towards the edge of the roof, but he skidded to a halt just in time, with his two front wheels hanging over the edge.

"I don't think I like this," thought poor Brum.

And then what do you think happened?

CLANG CLANG! "Out of the way! Clear a space!" CLANG CLANG!

Brum knew that noise. He peeped over the edge of the roof and saw a shiny red engine. It was his friends the firemen.

"Hang on, Brum!" shouted the people below. "Help is coming."

One of the firemen was holding a big bunch of balloons. Were they on their way to a party?

The firemen got out their longest ladder and propped it up against the tall building. Then the fireman with the balloons began to climb carefully up to Brum.

"I wonder if he's going to bring me some jelly and trifle as well," thought Brum. "What on earth is he up to?"

But the fireman had a very good idea.

"I'm going to tie these balloons to your radiator," said the fireman. "Now, I wonder how many it will need..."

"Need for what?" asked Brum. He was beginning to feel dizzy again.

"That should do it," said the fireman, tying on two more balloons.

As if by magic, Brum felt his two front wheels being lifted up by the balloons. Soon they were level with the roof, and he was able to reverse gently to safety.

"Now, would you like to float down?" laughed the fireman.

"No thanks," beeped Brum. "I'll leave that to the birds. But don't forget the doll and the balloon – that's why we're here."

The fireman carefully untangled the string from the satellite dish.

When Brum and the fireman appeared out of the building, the crowd of people who had been watching gave a huge cheer.

The little girl rushed up and gave Brum a big kiss on his bonnet, making his starting handle whiz round and round.

"Thank you, Brum, for saving my doll," she said. "And you too, Mr Fireman," she added, kissing the fireman who went very pink under his helmet.

The fireman gave the little girl the bunch of balloons. "We don't need these any more," he said. "Now climb up here with us and we'll give you a lift home."

As the fire engine drove along the streets, it passed the two bullies walking along the pavement.

The little girl waved at them, and they were so amazed to see her that they didn't watch where they were going. The next thing they knew, they were covered in dirty water. A man cleaning his car had thrown it in their path.

The little girl sat up in the fire engine with her doll and the balloons.

"This has turned out to be a lovely day," she said. "And it's all thanks to Brum. Look – there he is!"

Brum was speeding past them. The little girl waved and shouted, "I'll see you again, Brum."

But Brum didn't hear her. His engine was just too loud as he speeded off, brum brum brumming his way home.

Brum and the Fire Engine was first published by
HarperCollins Publishers in 1991
Second edition 1992

Text and Illustrations © HarperCollins Publishers 1991
Brum is a trademark of Ragdoll Productions Ltd
Licensed by Hit Licensing Initiatives

ISBN 0 00 664228 4

Printed and bound in Great Britain by Warners (Midlands) plc, Bourne + London

This book is set in Educentury